ISFENDIAR

and the
Bears of Mazandaran

Bronson Potter

ISFENDIAR

and the

Bears of Mazandaran

drawings by David Omar White

ATHENEUM 1969 NEW YORK

TO THE CHILDREN
OF ROXBURY, MASSACHUSETTS
where this story was written

ISFENDIAR
and the
Bears of Mazandaran

I

ISFENDIAR, THE CHARCOAL-BURNER'S SON, was restless. It had been an uneasy year in Melak, the last village on the edge of the great Iranian desert. The months of dry heat had taken all life from the plains and hills. He was fourteen, doing a man's work, but there was no meaning to it. Hot day followed hot day. The hours were dry shadows motionless near every rock. The beauty of creation seemed to have deserted the village and the desert. Isfendiar felt he needed adventure.

It seemed pointless to make charcoal that most people were too poor to buy. In previous years the village had had its share of good things. There had been the Year of the Rains, followed by the Year of the Wheat, when each field gave twice. Next came the Year of the Thorns, when Isfendiar had brought honor to his village by

3

capturing a wild donkey. Now they were in the Year of the Heat. The sun pressed hard on the hills. Each minute seemed to crackle with the thorns, and the days departed as slowly as unwelcome guests.

In the north, between the Elburz mountains and the Caspian Sea were the great forests of Mazandaran. In the lowlands next to the sea were the rice farms and the tropical fruit plantations. The great causeway of Shah Abbas ringed these rich lands that had been the playground of kings. Isfendiar knew that he had to see this part of his country. The mystery of the northern hills and mountains called to him like the voices in the charcoal-burner's poems. Isfendiar felt he would have to talk to his father about this wish for adventure.

One hot evening, after Isfendiar had stacked the day's charcoal with the charcoal of a hundred past days, he questioned his father.

"How is it I cannot do my work in peace, Patient One?" he asked, not getting the words to come out smoothly, but letting them tumble like stones down a slope.

The little gray-haired man was looking over the brickwork of one of his kilns. "As speaks the heart, so goes the man," he said in his quiet way. "For some time you have been restless. I could see it in the way your eyes sought the mountains. What can I say?"

"Have you nothing else to tell me, Honored One?" Isfendiar asked, using the formal mode of address in the way of a very young person speaking to an older.

After reflecting, the older man spoke again. "Maybe you can help me," he said slowly, still sorting the bricks. "Surely you will be able to help me, for you are still very young. My thoughts concern a child."

Isfendiar was silent, for he knew his father would speak wisdom.

"I shall put the question to you and ask that you let it live in your heart until the answer is ready to be heard."

"It shall be as you say, if God wills it."

"As God wills," the older man said gently. "The question is this: What do you say to a vain child, one who has been so blinded by his luck that he cannot find happiness?"

"Before God, that is not easy."

"I require that you do not attempt to answer," Isfendiar's father said, a little louder. "You must carry this question with you. When you have the answer, you must tell me, for I know such a child."

"Do I know the child?"

"Not as yet. But God willing, there is reason to believe that you will."

In the dog days of the year, the sun hung in the smoky sky so that even the gum bushes dropped and cracked. The gardens in the village were mere furrowed marks in the cracked mud. The wariest footstep raised clouds of dust to choke the walker. The men at the kilns spoke little. Charcoal was not bought, for there was little food to cook, and no house needed to be heated. Isfendiar's father piled his charcoal against better days. Each day fewer and fewer men walked up from the village to tend the fires. There was talk of old people dying in other villages. The talk had it that it was from the heat, but some said that it was hunger, for the grass was dead and the goats gave no milk. Charcoal was not bread, Isfendiar told himself. No matter how high a pile of charcoal he made for his father, he could not help to feed one mouth in the village. He must find his fortune elsewhere. The Patient One could not speak against sending money back from other places.

He would go north, Isfendiar decided. He had heard of Isphahan, the Halls of Jamshyd, Tehran, the mountains of the north and the sea at their feet. These places were written into the pages of the great poets. Here fortune lay, in the great bazaars, where every stall had richness from another part of the world.

"I am a charcoal-burner's son," Isfendiar said to himself. "The poorest of the poor. And in a bad year. But I have the name of a king, and I will seek adventure. I will see Mazandaran. I will put on my Bedouin knife and travel."

2

ISFENDIAR FOUND IT NOT SO HARD to get away from Melak as he had expected. The eyes of many were upon him; for if he found fortune, he would send money back for the village that was rapidly getting poorer and poorer.

The road to Neyriz, Isfendiar knew. He had his long knife, a few pieces of bread, a Kashkai hat, and canvas shoes to help his feet. The sense of adventure was not lessened by the endless stretches of rubbly road with not a speck of green to ease the eyes. At Duros a truck gave him a ride to the outskirts of Neyriz.

It took Isfendiar weeks to get north. He had the luck of falling in with a trader in Shiraz. The trader was from Bemzi. He had a new wife from one of the islands. She was tiny and wore a veil in the manner of the South. In the evening, when the veil came off, in the dimness of the firelight, Isfendiar saw why her father had sent her with so much jewelry. Her hair fell in neat ringlets even over the temples, her eyes seemed to peek out like the eyes of a forest animal. "We will have sons," said the trader. Then a little later, "and daughters, too." The girl from the islands giggled. During the ten days on the road to Isphahan, she did not speak to Isfendiar, or to any of the drovers. But she saved bits of suet for those whose lips cracked in the sun.

In Isphahan, there was work on the beet trucks, but none seemed to pay enough to let Isfendiar send money home. Each day, he had enough for a little food, and that was all. It seemed very hard, working and having nothing left over. Isfendiar tried to be patient.

He found himself in Tehran, then in Shemiran, where there were rich people. He worked in the garden of a man who threw him a rial for what seemed to Isfendiar just ordinary courtesy. "You must come from the country, to be so well spoken," the rich man said. The rial Isfendiar sent by post to his father. It would buy bread in the village.

In Shemiran, Isfendiar heard of a busload of pilgrims going to Tabriz. He took a job as helper to the driver of the bus. He had only to look after things when the driver slept at night and sometimes do a little work with the tools. Once he spent all night blowing up a tire with a leaky pump.

In Tabriz Isfendiar found himself taken on by a group making up for a hunt. There were four city men. They had fine clothes and shiny rifles, and seemed too fat for climbing in the mountains.

The four city men had a guide by the name of Haidar. He was a thin, tall man with a little beard on his chin, and he carried an ancient musket. He was a mountain man who had come to Tabriz with a load of rice from Mazandaran, the province by the Caspian Sea. Haidar had talked the four hunters into trying their luck in Mazandaran, on the slopes of the Elburz, where the hunting was famous. There were wild pig, deer and sheep, wolves, bear and many small animals. The Elburz were the thrones of kings, Haidar said. Who had not marveled at the great Mount Demavend? And who had not heard of the Throne of Solomon thrusting its pinnacle into the northern skies? "I know of such things from Saadi, the poet," Isfendiar told Haidar, "Saadi, the wandering poet of Shiraz."

They took a truck back towards Tehran. At Karaj they turned north and in a day were at a little town called Gach I Sar. The truck managed to take them to a little village up the mountain trail from Gach I Sar. There were mules to be had the following morning, brought up from the farms below. Bearers also, when mention of money was made. Many of the bearers were carrying rice across the passes in anticipation of winter, but there were also a few resting who could be persuaded to work for money.

There was an old stable with pallets, which passed for a hotel. On the door were painted the ancient signs

9

of the stopping place of the caravan.

When the truck had been unloaded and all the equipment locked in the stable, Haidar bargained with a passing townsman for cuts of northern lamb. "Watch, Southlander," he told Isfendiar. "You will learn how we cook in the mountains."

Haidar leaned his old musket against a wall and put his hat over the barrel. He gathered together some scraps of wood and struck fire with two stones from his belt. When the fire was brisk, Haidar covered it with flat rocks so the fire could only creep through the cracks.

After a while, Haidar took a square chip of wood and flipped one of the rocks so it flew clear of the fire. From his belt he took a little tallow wrapped in a sheep's in-

testine, and held the intestine over the hot stone so the tallow dripped down. There was sizzling and the smoke caught fire, but the fat on the stone did not burn. "Just right, Southlander," said Haidar. "This is how we cook in the mountains." The tall man threw the cuts of meat onto the hot stone. Smoke rose into the air like offerings to the gods.

In a little while, Haidar pressed the steaks with the chip so they sizzled more, then flipped them onto another rock he had prepared the same way as the first. In a moment, Isfendiar had a piece of meat before him on a chip. He looked wonderingly at Haidar, but the older man was already eating his piece in his fingers. "Eat," said the older man. "If you do not, the gods will know you are not hungry, and they will take the joy out of the thing."

Steam rose enticingly from the piece of meat that now was browned delicately so that the marbled fat drew away a little from the lean. Still, it was so hot that Isfendiar could not touch it easily. He watched Haidar toss down the last fragment of the other piece, clean his fingers magically in a little sand, throw the sand into the fire so no devil would find it, belch lustily into the wind, then twist a bit of tobacco from his belt. All in an instant. "A bit of that newspaper I saw you poring over, I beg thee, Honored Lord," said Haidar using the familiar, humorously imitating a beggar. With the newspaper he made a little rectangle appear from the edge, without marring the print. The tobacco was crushed in one hand,

11

the paper worked into the palm of the other so the tobacco could be pressed into it, and magically made into
a finished cigarette with the help of a wet tongue. "Your
meat cools, young friend," said Haidar, as he put a coal
to the end of the cigarette in his mouth.

In the way of the South, Isfendiar felt shy eating before someone not of his family. Haidar seemed to sense
this and put his back against a rock facing north. He
talked as Isfendiar ate.

"We should have a melon to go with our meat,"
Haidar said. "Not one of these stingy shriveled lowland
melons, but one from the Caspian people. A little one,
round, and kept cool."

"It would be good," Isfendiar said, without really
thinking. Melons were an absurdity for people as poor
as they were.

"But melon sellers are all thieves," Haidar said, warm-
ing to the story for which he had formed an audience.
"They put themselves where you cannot resist their
wares, and then charge you three times the going price."

"Is it true?" asked Isfendiar. He had never found himself cheated by a seller of fruits, even an Armenian.

"Why, child, surely you are making fun of me! Why
I knew a melon seller who was the most terrible bandit
you could imagine. His name was Saadi, the same as the
poet. And he came from Kasvin. He kept a long Bedouin
knife under his pile of melons. When a stranger came to
buy, Saadi would find out all about him and offer his
melons for next to nothing. Then he would follow the

stranger and rob him. And he would not hesitate to use the knife. He bought himself camels and became rich. He bought a beautiful wife, had many children all of whom went to the University in Tehran."

And as at the end of a typical mountain story, the teller was smugly silent, for the story was like a seed that would blossom within the hearer of its own accord. Isfendiar had a sense of being made the fool. Robbers should not be able to buy beautiful wives. They should not have camels and send their children to the University. Why, then, did Haidar, a poor man, say things like this?

"Eater of Hashish," Isfendiar said to his friend, "I love the clown in you more than I love the hunter. You would not leave this way of life if you could."

And Haidar laughed, the loud rich laugh of the mountain man, when there was no fear of being overheard. "For a Southlander you are not so silly," he said. "Not so silly, anyway, as the fake men who carry ten-inch knives at their sides."

"I carry such a knife," said Isfendiar sensing that he was being drawn in again. "Maybe you had not noticed, Haidar of the Marvelous Musket."

"Such a big knife, and such a little man," Haidar chuckled. "We will have great deeds."

"It serves to cut my meat," said Isfendiar.

"I will keep my chickens hid, with you in town," Haidar said. "My rifle is no match for such a thing."

"It is the custom of the South," Isfendiar said.

13

"I made jest," Haidar said. "It was not to trouble you."

"It was not trouble. I thought you did not understand, you being hidden in the mountains all your life." Isfendiar was conscious of the game swinging slowly his way.

"I have been to Meshed," said Haidar, not laughing so much.

"And did the dealers in the bazaar take advantage of your mountain manners? Is this where the story of Saadi comes from?"

"Ah," said Haidar sadly. "It is as you say. I lost many toman in the bazaar. To a seller of silver things."

"Never mind," said Isfendiar. "Next time I will accompany you, and point out your mistakes. When you walk with a Southlander, you walk with a wise man."

"You have bested me, Little Friend," said Haidar. And he laughed his great mountain laugh as if nothing in the world pleased him so much.

3

IN THE MORNING HAIDAR FOUND MULES and drivers,
two other mountain men, and five bearers. "These are
rich men," he said to Isfendiar. "It will take an army to
carry their tents and their blankets." But the mountain
man was cheerful enough, and before the sun was very
high in the sky, they had set off up the mountain trail
towards a tiny mountain village called Tosh.

Isfendiar walked with Haidar at the head of the col-
umn. The city men rode mules behind, and the bearers
and luggage mules came last. As they walked Haidar
talked of what there was to expect in the mountains.
Particularly he talked of Tosh, a village he knew well.
Haidar talked and talked. And Isfendiar listened.

Near Tosh, Haidar said, the village in the mountains,
there was a hut for people going across the passes. Tosh

15

was but a tiny, poor village, yet the villagers kept the hut, for there was a common sympathy for those who had to deal with the snow and the passes.

In the forenoon they passed near the peak of a small mountain called Hill of Woe. Haidar made Isfendiar come with him to the peak while the others followed the trail. In a small plateau looking up to the sky a field had been made by turning up rocks in a circle as large as one could throw a stone across. In this field there were a thousand sticks bearing small brass ornaments like bells. And brass hands hammered out of crude metal, some eaten away by the weather, but all pointing at the sky.

"These are the mysteries of the mountains," Haidar said. "These things were put here by ghosts. The old women in many towns have seen the mountain devils and seen their prints in the snow. The goatherders talk of wraiths high in the summer grazing lands. And spells cast by demons so that your foot will surely stumble." He looked narrowly at Isfendiar. "How do you like these things, Southlander?" he asked closely.

"I know little, Honored Friend. I must reflect on what I have seen and what you have told me."

"That is well said," Haidar said. And in his abrupt way he turned and strode off down the mountain, taking such long strides that Isfendiar had to struggle to keep up.

"To make a hunt you must have guides, bearers and a camp boy," Haidar said later in the afternoon. "The camp boy must do his work and keep to himself. If he is of different religion from the others, he must keep to himself when he prays. He must keep his ideas to himself. To the others the camp boy is nothing: he is next to dirt; it is he who must deal with the charcoal-burners and the goatherders. The camp boy must make tea from the thick water carried in goatskins and bring dry sugar to put in it. And though he must do all the shoes and boots at night, his hands must be clean enough to serve the hunters their breakfast. His courage must not fail on the patches of ice in the mountains, and he must not tremble at the sound of the bears. He must serve with loyalty and be paid next to nothing.

"Yet the camp boy is everything in a hunting party," Haidar said. "If he is cheerful and does his duties with pleasure, it can change the mood of the group. If no task is too small for him to pursue with diligence and interest —and after all, this is only love for his masters in its finest form—then somehow the hunt goes better come fortune, fair or foul. But if he is sullen or cannot keep the boots greased against the morning wet, then there are accidents, and accidents in the mountains often mean death."

Haidar measured his words. "In the camp the hunters keep apart from the bearers and the guides. In the evening, when the cup of the sky silently twists about the world, the hunters drink their expensive wine and talk of big game. The bearers and the guides listen to the little noises of the night and wonder what the fortune of the next day will bring. For them there is tea and the huge Persian breads like elephants' ears. If there has been shooting, good red meat will make the walking easy.

"If the eyes of the hunters look at one another in happiness and friendship then the eyes of the bearers may seek their own kind of happiness: the dim light of the horizon, the lakes lying under the sky. For to them this is the music of life, opening their eyes to God's works. The hunt is for them no week's entertainment; it is a way of life, and the dangers make it all the more beautiful. All have heard stories of the bears that will slip into camp at night and destroy the food. And even more, the wraiths that one must see before one is seen so one can spit to keep off the evil."

"You carry the blood of poets in you, too," said Isfendiar to his new friend. They were climbing a scarp with shaley rock that clogged the footsteps and made noises like broken crockery.

"I give you not a penny for your Hafiz and your Saadi, Southlander," said Haidar. "I am my own poet, a mountain man. When I talk, women and children listen."

"I will listen to you while you talk," said Isfendiar, "but I will listen to the poet when the poet sings."

Haidar went on about the life in the mountains and on the hunt. "Sometimes in the early morning a hunting party will stumble across goatherders who have moved their herds high to escape the summer dryness. Then the guides and bearers will sit in at the herders' fire while the hunters wait. One of the guides will light a cigarette and pass it around the circle. All will smoke from the same cigarette, and when it has returned to the man who offered it, the talk will begin.

"The talk is always of the same things: first of water, then of wheat. For these mountain men have their souls with their home tribes. Then of love and death, how their women love and how they fare on their mission. Next of things at hand. It is then that the guides can ask of game."

The sun had dipped behind the peaks to the southwest when the hunting party arrived at Tosh. The dogs barked and nipped at the mules, the bearers cursed, and the townspeople made signs to ward off the evil eye. But the chief of the tribe made his house available to the hunters. The bearers found quarters where they could. Isfendiar put his things in the storage shed behind the chief's tea house.

4

IN THE MORNING THEY SET OFF up the path to the northwest. They were to skirt the range of mountains and dip into the forests of Mazandaran. From there they would return into the mountains, driving the game before them. Now they had no mules, only bearers. They carried only what they needed, for the way was hard. Isfendiar himself had to carry a canvas bag of the hunters' clothes.

In the evening they set up camp on the northern slope of a mountain for which no name was known. Isfendiar had to make the fire and do some of the cooking. The bearers kept him busy with their cries for bread and the meats cooked on the fire. They would have to kill soon Haidar said, or be out of meat.

That night Isfendiar dreamed of the wild donkeys of

22

the plains he had left far to the south. By foot and by truck he had made his way to the north. He had a thick coating of dust all over him. But he had arrived. And now he was in the eternal Elburz.

In the morning, as he turned to the east to remember the way in which All was made, he spoke with the God of wild animals and the eternal hills. For a moment Isfendiar thought that he understood the beckoning brass hands on the mountain peak.

During the night the clouds had descended so that the going was difficult. Writhing rivers of fog streaked along every slope, and the vegetation smelled of decay. At noon a little sun came out, but not enough to track by. "We will have better luck tomorrow," Haidar said.

But the hunters were uneasy. They had come a long way for this trip, they said, and they had not counted on bad weather. For the rest of the day, they advanced carefully along the slippery rock. That night the fires fluttered dismally in the wetness. There was fog everywhere. The flames looked as though the wood had come from the sea, eerie blue flames that had not the heat to burn a piece of meat. And when the water boiled, it was not hot.

The next day the mountains were still in clouds, and the sun never broke through. Early the next morning, one of the bearers slipped on a shaley slope, and it took a good hour to get him back on his feet, and walking with the group. "It is not as it should be," said one of the hunters. "We walk for nothing. Oh yes, there are

23

sheep here, and goats. But they can hear us coming for hours before we arrive. They laugh at us. They eat their fill, and when they fill their desire they make their way into hiding." The bearers were gloomy, and at lunchtime Haidar gave them tobacco to lend them heart.

"It is a bad season," one of the hunters said in the evening. "We sweat all day. We do nothing. There is the fog, and we sweat all day. It is October. We sweat during the day, in the fog. And at night, we could have snow. Much of it. There is no game. We will have fog for weeks, and it could snow. It is bad."

That night they heard a sound of animals. It was a low pig-like sound at first, the sound of animals eating. Then there was a new sound, the fierce cry of jealousy and blood lust.

"Bears," said Haidar, speaking softly to Isfendiar so the hunters could not overhear. "They will find our camp if we do not move. And then we will have no peace. Bears can be ugly."

The next day, try as they would, they could move only slowly on the slippery rocks. The hunters were angry. "You call yourselves guides," they said. "We see no game. And you insist on going on. If there is nothing but bear, we will hunt bear."

"It is not that there are no sheep," Haidar told the hunters, "they are all around us. During the day, you will hear a stone rattle, and you will know there are sheep above. But you cannot see them in this fog. The gods are not with us. The bearers slip on the wet stones. They

cannot breathe as they should in this fog. At night they cough and cannot sleep. And the bears. Each night they come closer. They smell our bread and meat. But it will be better. This fog cannot last."

The hunters said they did not believe Haidar. They made him post guard that night. Each man would watch for two hours by the stars.

In spite of the guard, a hamper of food was missing the next morning. It was the hamper with the leftovers the hunters gave to the bearers. No one said anything about bears, just that the hamper was missing. All that day they tried to scale a slope on the north side of the mountain called The Elk, but the rock was wet and slippery, and the fog pressed so upon them that they missed a traverse and had to bed down on a muddy ledge a good two hours journey from camp.

That night the dawn guard fired at a wall above them to the west. "Two big shapes up there," he said. But when the other men looked at the wall, they said it was impossible. Nothing living could be there. The fellow was dreaming. He had the mountain sickness, when visions come before the eyes.

Isfendiar listened and said nothing. He had never before seen such things. He was not frightened, exactly, yet the tales the men told of bear before going to sleep had a flavor about them that stayed with you the whole night. The tales made a bearer turning over in his sleep sound like an army of heavy footed animals.

Isfendiar noticed that the bearers slept uneasily now,

26

and that they tired during the day. They made slow progress. "It is the air," said Haidar. "Little food and thin air. They worry. Listen to them at night. Before they sleep, they sound like a school full of frightened children. The wraiths of the night haunt them. If things do not improve they will start deserting us."

The next day, it was just as Haidar said. A man called Yali, a puny worthless sort, sneaked out of camp in the early morning. "He will not get down by himself," Haidar said, and shouted into the fogbank for him to come back. There was no reply from the churning fog. Haidar's voice came back empty and plaintive from the foggy caverns that belonged to another world.

The next night they lit fires against the bears. The big animals prowled unhappily in the rocks that surrounded the camp.

"They are hungry," Haidar said. "We may have to shoot tomorrow night, unless the fog lifts."

The next day dawned uneasily, with the sky taking a full hour to gain the color of heated lead. The fog swirled through the rocks, and when the bearers went to put on their loads, the water dripped down the leather thongs and the canvas headpieces. By noon they had given up the idea of moving far. The ropy fog swirled around their legs, greasing the rocks. They were in a chimney that led to a small peak, and the fog seemed to pour down the chimney as in a funnel. They ate their noon meal in silence sitting at a large tablestone tilted precariously over a deep gulley.

As they ate, Isfendiar was conscious of a strange sound from the slopes below. It was a muffled noise as if someone had a pillow and was beating it against a rod. Isfendiar noticed that Haidar was listening also. The others seemed not to hear. The noise quieted for a while, then there was a terrible cry, a long hollow bleating wail. Isfendiar had heard the same noise from his goats when a hyena got among them. He looked at Haidar inquiringly.

"It is those bears again. This time they are killing sheep," Haidar said almost in a whisper. He looked shaken.

"But bear do not kill animals," Isfendiar said.

"They kill sheep," said the guide. "They eat meat."

"What are you whispering about?" one of the hunters wanted to know.

"It is time to start," Haidar said to the hunter. "Dusk will be upon us if we do not start."

"These bears that you hear killing sheep," Haidar said later to Isfendiar, "they make no trouble. And even the ones that come into camp and steal. If you have fire, it is nothing. But I have heard that there is one called the Bear of Shuttra Khan that ranges near Salambar Pass, not too far from where we may go. This one goes everywhere, on the mountains, on the Elburz glacier, and in the forests. It has been wounded many times by hunters and their dogs. It has killed men, and wounded others to death. The men speak of tattered ears and a white crescent on its chest. Now this is strange, because many of the bears have a crescent moon of lighter hair on their chests, but this one, the hair is snowy white. The men of Syalen and Arud say that if you see this white you will not live."

"Superstition," Isfendiar said. "The tales of old women. In the South the old women talk of bandits, but men do not walk in fear." Still, the tone of his voice did not bear out his words. The words came out chilled and frosty, just as Haidar's words had sounded in his heart.

"The winter before this last winter the Bear of Shuttra Khan killed some penned sheep near Arud, and one of the men shot at it with a rifle. It was a hunting rifle, no toy such as the musket I carry. And the bullets did nothing. The bear killed the man. His friends found him with twenty cartridges beside him."

"We have no such things in the South," Isfendiar said with a shudder. "Only the desert, which is a friend to the men who respect it."

The bearers were uneasy to the point of recklessness. In the late afternoon one of them slipped and sprained his ankle. Even after his ankle was bound, he had to use a stick. The other bearers were then terrified and did not want to walk the slopes. That evening they spent in a small hollow. All evening they could hear the bears pulling bark from the trees far below in the woods.

The next day they did not move. They could only watch the wall of fog. The bears would be quiet for a few minutes, and then the noise would start again, booming hollowly up from below. The time dragged. If a man breathed heavily, it sounded like heavy paws on the rocks. Isfendiar would turn, only to be facing a wall of fog, which the glow of the fire made move in a fantastic fashion.

Then it seemed to Isfendiar that the fog was clearing. Sure enough, by late afternoon, patches of sky were visible. A little wind came up, and as it increased little pellets of ice blew into the camp. Isfendiar put some more wood on the fire, as if this would halt the snow that was sure to come.

In the evening, even before the campfires had burned down, a piercing north wind blew in from the direction of Zen ad Kind. The upper air was startlingly clear. White wisps and streamers of clouds caught the departing sunlight and shed an uneasy shadowless light on the tableland. No hint of the warm summer was here now. The goatherders were long gone, hidden in their sod huts far below. The hunters in their hide coats were as bizarre and out-of-place as a peasant child in the great room of the Peacock Throne. From a peak of a distant mountain, to the west, a winter streamer of white flew like a hideous little flag. Snow, all the men muttered. There will be snow.

Yet, to the north, in the countless valleys and tortured passageways the warm evening fog came all the same. It seemed to blow in on the same Caspian wind and mount as uneventfully as water flowing into a pond. Looking at it, the eye could not see it move.

Isfendiar found a rock with a little trench on the uphill side. He would sleep there, where he was at least partly sheltered from the wind and where the flank of the rock would reflect the heat from his fire.

But when it came time to gather wood, it was hard to swell his meager pile. There was little light. At length, he found a shrub in the lee of an outcropping. He could pretend he had a fire, anyway.

Isfendiar was to stand guard until the tenth hour, when the sign of the Bear had turned toward Demavend. While the others slept, Isfendiar piled some rocks to make a little oven. Maybe in the morning they could make a hoe-cake.

Before the head of the Bear had turned a fraction, it seemed, the moon came up in the east to show the Caspian mists roiled like enormous ocean waves, slow and as powerful as the winds that pushed them.

The mists had risen above the tree line, but in the wind a bank would dip back to reveal a dark ravine, then spring forward again to lash the craggy slopes.

The sky, too, was troubled. No sooner had the moon revealed herself, than it was partly obscured with flat clouds that scudded angrily to the southern horizon, so that the Great Dog and the Lesser Dog were soon obscured.

It was too early for such weather. Yet in the South they would be cursing the dryness and waiting for the fall rains. Maybe these very clouds would be those that wet the edges of the great desert. Or maybe green Shemiran took its strength from these Caspian clouds. A month earlier, he had been entranced by the white cap on Mount Demavend. Now he was a part of the white North. He would have tales to tell when he returned to the South, Isfendiar thought. Strange how dreamlike his home and the warm South seemed in this lonely waste.

A little later, Isfendiar heard a foreign, rattling noise from the direction of the sleeping guides. Investigating, he saw nothing. But, as he turned to leave, he heard the noise come again. It seemed to come from the cooking pot; and as he looked, he heard the noise again.

The broth in the pot, so warm an hour before, had cooled and even as he watched was icing over. As Isfendiar contemplated this wonder, an insect brushed his cheek.

The tips of his fingers sweeping against the intruder met astonishing cold. Isfendiar looked to his left and saw what he had heard described but had never seen before. The moonlight was clouded with what looked like a million million infinitesimal white leaves, sparkling and whirling. It was snow.

The snows came as the warring tribes of mankind. The Medes, Lurs, the Fars and Persians. All history was written there. As the flakes contested each other in billowing gusts, they fell finally onto the curtain that now shielded the ground with nothing to mark where they lay. Where were now the glories of the warrior? Where were now the royal pennants that had been followed? Where were now the great wishes for conquest, the empires, the things to be done? The snow fell, and carpeted

over itself. Were men's goals such as these? Must all rest under the snow? Where were the heroes of years gone by?

Isfendiar heard one of the men grunt, then call out a name. One of the bearers, dreaming of his village. The name could be that of his dog, "Hanaha." Another man cursed the dreamer, and the camp was left to the sounds of the wind. Was death this way? Could a man only try to take what he could from another man, then join the grains in the desert sands?

"You should have waked me."

Isfendiar felt a hand on his shoulder. It was Hoomah, one of the bearers from Tosh. Isfendiar had slept. No, he had not slept, he had been dreaming while the moon spun through the sky.

"I thought not to call you," Isfendiar said.

"There is much snow."

"It . . . it is very strange."

"You are a Southlander?"

"The same."

"You should grease your lips, then."

"I have heard as much. I will go, now, Strong Hoomah."

"Goodnight, Southlander."

"Goodnight, Hoomah."

34

5

IN THE MORNING THE MEN COUGHED and cursed as they
rolled out of their blankets. They had been transformed
into old men by the cold. Their hair and beards were
white. But Haidar was happy. "We will find game," he
said. "Good, easy tracking."

"He is a madman," one of the hunters said. "He
wants to risk the lives of respectable men for his profit.
You will see. We will have to climb this pinnacle or that
one to look for game. And a little slip will mean death."

"I know nothing of these things, Honored Friend,"
Isfendiar said. "But I can listen to your wisdom."

Haidar wanted to cross back to the chimney and climb
into the saddle of the two mountains. As they worked
their way across the rocky traverse, the cry of an angered,
injured animal came from the slopes below. "Not wolf,"

Haidar said. "A wolf is intelligent and quick. It is the bear who is sloppy and can only kill by biting off a hindquarter. We will see more of them, these bears, and this one with the bloodlust."

In the afternoon, they came across the tracks of a few wild sheep. Much of the snow had melted, but the patches that remained clearly showed the sheep moving toward the north side of the mountain called the Elder, the side protected from the wind coming off the sea many miles away.

"They will spend the evening hours in the lee of that bluff," Haidar told the hunters.

The bearers put down their loads. Haidar took the hunters and started out on the long trek across the flank of the Elder. Isfendiar was to follow with the extra cartridges and things for cleaning the game. The hunters walked in silence.

Almost at sundown they came on five or six sheep standing almost exactly where Haidar had said they would be. The hunters fired and brought one down. Another was wounded, and Isfendiar noticed that it was Haidar who scaled the crest to where the wounded sheep had run.

In the evening they ate early and rolled into blankets right away. In the night one of the bearers cried out as if in fear. It was a nightmare. In the morning, Haidar said: "We face our own demons." The bears frightened Haidar, one of the men said; but to Isfendiar, who had seen frightened men before, Haidar seemed unchanged,

the same leathery face giving the same terse commands. The bears were still there. They could be heard every night, but they were further down the slope, and they seemed to have found something that kept them away from the camp.

The next day the hunting was good, and the hunters said they would stay up in the mountains, more snow or not. Now they could not be talked into going down. Haidar said the supplies were running short and any night could bring more snow. But the hunters wanted bigger trophies. Each evening showed new larger animals alongside the fire, and the hunters were happy.

The days went by quickly, the hunting taking up most of the daylight hours and the keeping of the camp the few minutes that remained. The group skirted the flank of a mountain called by an old-fashioned Turkish name from the days of the invasion. They passed from spur to spur, getting farther from the trail that led to the lowlands and to safety. The hunting made them forget the snow. Far away to the north the sun still shone on warm forests. Once Isfendiar thought he could see the sea lying under great banks of billowing fog, but more frequently all he could see were the clouds that lay below them now and the cavernous sides of mountains in the distance. Far away, oh so far away, were the dry hills of the South, the charcoal kilns of his family, the village where he was known, and the house where had had been born.

Tragedy struck soon enough. A bearer, slipping in a

rocky crevice hidden under the snow, fell and broke a leg. Haidar was suddenly furious. "We are fools," he cried. "Playing at the tops of mountains where only the gods can breathe. Now see what has come. The man cannot walk. Only if the snow melts, can we get him down. If the snow does not melt . . ."

They waited a day, then another. There was no more hunting, though the hunters grumbled for it. Each night the snow fell. At his watch, Isfendiar would feel the snow blow out of the peaks of the mountains; then as the blackness lightened, the snow would cease and the stars come out once more. This meant that the clouds were below. Sometimes Isfendiar would spend his watch looking for the light of a village below; but in all the time he was in the mountains, he saw no light. The world below did not exist. They were the only people in the world, in snowy crags encircled by bears.

November had passed, and the stormy month was there. The mountain top caches of brass hands were covered. The season's snow was upon them. And they had a man with a broken leg. He had become the employer, a guest really, and they his servants. They were to get him down.

Haidar, usually the most cautious and the most respectful of the forces of nature, took on a mad cheerfulness. He talked of a Christian in Meshed who being known as a fool made it a part of his philosophy. "The Christian said that it was true that the Virgin had smiled on him and made him a fool," Haidar said. "It was hard, sometimes, but all the same he would have no other life, no other world, no other God.".

Still, it was December, and the snows were there to stay. The fact that the bears had not gone into caves did not mean that the snow would melt. Each night brought more snow. The crags had disappeared. The hard mountains were clothed in soft whiteness. Everywhere was nothingness. You could not walk. There was nothing to keep your eyes on when you tried to move. It was bad. The injured man would have to be carried down through the ever-growing snowbanks.

"You have snow sickness," Haidar said, looking at Isfendiar. "It is nothing, as long as you keep moving. But if you are by yourself, it is bad. I have come upon hunters just sitting and looking out at the world of snow. If you are by yourself, you have to take things out of your pocket and rearrange them and count the people in your house below. Now be a good boy, and do as I tell you; for I feel that I will have need of you, not as a camp boy, but as a trusted servant. If you start thinking strange things, make some task for yourself. Clean your boots, or polish your knife. Then the soul will not be frightened of becoming lost, and it will stay strong to help you. These bears, they are nothing, they can only kill you. But in the early hours of the morning, when you are on watch, then the spirit is the feeblest, and it is then you must help it to live. Spit if you see demons."

The next day, Isfendiar found out what Haidar had meant about needing him. They were to go to a village below, Isfendiar and Haidar. Haidar would not go alone, and he would have to leave all the other men in camp to take care of the hunters and the injured man.

"Do you want a rifle?" Haidar asked Isfendiar. "There will be danger."

"The gazelle has no cudgel," Isfendiar said, meaning that his fleetness of foot depended on not carrying anything heavy.

"A pistol, then?"

"A worthless tool, good only to deprive another man of his life. I will wear my knife like a Southlander. That is enough to give my heart courage. And I can make use of it the way a humble man does, to eat with and to cut his way through the underbrush."

So it was set. Haidar and Isfendiar were to go to one of the mountain villages to fetch men, a litter, and food. They would return within a week. Meanwhile the hunting party would once again shoot sheep, this time to feed itself, and the injured man could rest. His leg was splinted, and he was not in too much pain. He whimpered at night, though, and said that Haidar was going to desert them all and leave them to the bears.

Isfendiar, before he left, made a little amulet from dried grass and left it with the injured man. "You will keep it for me, friend," he said. "It will do me good knowing you have it with you. You will pray for us; and when I return with the bearers, you can give it back to me." After that, the injured man seemed easier in his mind and called out to be fed and taken care of.

6

IN THE MORNING, THEY SET OUT. Haidar, carrying a rifle and a small pack, led the way. Isfendiar carried meat for one day and the bread that could be spared in camp. They would shoot as they went, and they could stop to melt snow for water.

Haidar plunged down the snowy slope as though he knew every inch of the way. Isfendiar had to stop and cut himself a stick to probe the snow with. Twice he almost lost his footing, so that he feared he might slide over a ridge. Haidar, understandably enough, could not spare time to help his companion. Isfendiar could only try to keep to Haidar's footprints and hope for the best.

The sun on the snow was the worst thing, Isfendiar found. When it was at its worst, it reflected off the clouds and the snow, so as to be almost blinding.

42

All day they descended, Haidar with his half-running, lumbering gait; Isfendiar with blood in his ears, his lungs bursting and a dryness in his throat that tortured like the desert sun. Finally, Haidar, below the forest line, threw his rifle on the ground and said, "Here. We will sleep. Make a fire while I find some pine boughs for shelter."

Isfendiar caught his breath and gathered some wood.

That night they stood no watches. "We need our sleep," Haidar said. "If the bears want us, they are welcome, as long as they do not wake us."

But sleep did not come to Isfendiar. After all the exertion and meager food, sleep came only in a trickle, a thin shadowy kind of sleep, in which the loneliness of the slopes and the infinity of space and stars drained the comfort from the warmth of the blankets. Isfendiar dreamed again and again of ugly things, monsters so small they could disappear behind pebbles.

In the morning, when the sky first lightened, Isfendiar's eyes opened, whether in dream or truth, he knew not, and he saw a huge black shape pawing one of the pines at the edge of their little camp. Isfendiar seized a brand from the fire and threw it. The shape slipped into the forest and disappeared, and Isfendiar's eyes closed again watching the smoke from the brand make a little river flowing upward into the lightening sky.

"I heard the noise," Haidar said when he woke up. "You need not have bothered. We have no food worth touching; and unless a killer bear gets here, we are all right. The killer we know nothing about. A robber will storm into camp. He touches no tree bark. If we were not so tired at night, we could watch. It will be no more than three days, and we will have help."

The next day they threw themselves into the great forests above the valley of the plains. Water was running everywhere, dripping through the trees, collecting into small streams on the banks, then roaring through the stream beds that had been dry when they climbed up. Late in the morning, Haidar halted and waited for Isfendiar to catch up. "Look behind you," he said.

Isfendiar looked, could see nothing out of the ordinary. There were the mountains, the purple haze, the clouds above them, the streamers of fog from the peaks, nothing else.

"Look closer," Haidar said, his voice direct and commanding.

Isfendiar looked at the trail they had come down. His eyes swept up the mountainside through the forest. He listened to Haidar's voice drumming in his ear. "Look hard, and you will see." And finally, a mere thousand feet from where they stood, he saw the shadow. "A shadow, I see a shadow," Isfendiar said.

He felt Haidar's friendly hand on his shoulder. The hand bit him a little to tell him he had not seen correctly.

"Look again," said Haidar. "Use your eyes, and tell me what you see."

Isfendiar put his eyes to the same spot, saw the

shadow move slowly, ponderously, saw the size of it, and in an instant his brain filled in what his eyes had not seen before. It was a bear, a huge, loping, mountain of a bear. And it was coming down their trail, sniffing its way, to make up for the eyes that could see only dimly.

Haidar evidently sensed Isfendiar's surprise with what he saw. "Yes," he said, "it could be the killer of Shuttra Khan. I have heard men speak of him. And we are lucky if it is he, for we have seen him. Otherwise we could have camped and not known about him. And he has probably followed for two days. We will kill him or he will kill us. It might be that he will find a sheep, but I doubt it at these altitudes. And probably now that he is following us, he would let a sheep go right under his nose without touching it. Tonight, when the sun is down, we will set up an ambush. Maybe we will be able to kill it. If not, we will have to get much wood and keep a fire going all night. These mountains are haunted. It is as if this bear is a spirit, not a real bear that should be eating bark and berries."

And Isfendiar sensed what Haidar was talking about. The dark mountains, without a sign of habitation, the streams of fog that seemed to drip from everywhere, the muffled echoes of their steps, the glistening droplets of water on every rock, the ghostly trees wreathed in mist, and the trickle of unseen waters behind all the rocks and in every small gully. The place smelled of death, of decay. Even as he talked with Haidar, the bear, as if feeling their eyes, disappeared.

"We will not see him again until the ambush," Haidar said. "He is wise, this old bear. He has made fools of many men. Maybe he will make fools of us. Who can tell? If we only had some dogs. Well, no matter. God's will is God's will."

"So be it under God," said Isfendiar, responding in the manner of the South. He was glad to see Haidar smile, relax his face, and swing down the slope again, the bear forgotten, at least for the moment.

It was the dreams that worried Isfendiar as he tagged along behind Haidar, trying to keep the pace without puffing too hard. He knew about men's dreams, for his father had told him, the dreams that came in loneliness and in desolate places. But these dreams that had their heart in the endless winter snows of the mountain tops plagued his days and made his nights so restless he awoke feeling that he had just come in from the kilns and needed a night on the dry floor of the family hut to make him whole again.

In the early afternoon they crossed to a scarp running northeast into the forest. In the distance it looked as though the snow was light there, that the wind maybe had blown it clear, or the last sun of the day before had lightened it.

But when they arrived they found snow and the scarp throwing itself in steep screes into the valley, so that they could not pass that way.

It was late in the afternoon when they got back to the north foothills of Elburz al Kain. They were above the

47

trees again. Haidar made Isfendiar take a bit of light rope and go ahead so that Haidar could check him in case of accident. "We are tired," said Haidar. "Who knows what can happen? And I like not the look of your lowland shoes."

Isfendiar did feel himself tiring. With the shadows long, the eyes tired in seeking out places for the feet to step safely. And the air did not have the fragrance of lowland air. Here it was thin and dry so that you had to swallow to keep your throat wet. The eyes smarted and watered, and the skin around the nose grew dry and pinched.

He could feel Haidar keeping at gauge length on the little bit of rope, and it seemed strange that they should be two men on the endless snow, sent back from a day in which they had gained nothing.

Late in the day Haidar went up a little slope so as to keep in the fading light. As he climbed a bank to a plateau, he crossed their tracks from early that morning. There they were, the large prints from Haidar's canvas boots and Isfendiar's smaller prints.

Isfendiar's eyes followed the footprints to where they went over an outcropping. Two small boulders contained the path they had followed. The sun had melted the snow cap on one of the boulders. Isfendiar's eyes saw, pondered, swept the slope, then returned.

The rock had changed since that morning. As he ran to question Haidar, his eyes saw the extra trail in the snow. His heart jumped into his throat.

It was the trail of the five fingers. The cursed bear again. As Isfendiar turned, he felt that Haidar no longer held the rope. His eyes first saw the older man some feet behind, halted with his rifle cradled in one arm. He was looking up at the table rock, and as he sensed that Isfendiar turned, he tilted his head back slightly in the universal sign for caution.

Isfendiar halted and crouched. His eyes scanned all. Finally Haidar's voice came. "We will see nothing. He is too clever for us."

Haidar walked by, strode up the path onto the little plateau. Isfendiar was left alone to struggle after. He was very tired.

Back again in the strange world of the mountains, with the fog and the snow blowing through the fields of sticks with the brass hands at their tops, the bearers' accidents and the hunters' endless quest for game seemed trivial. In it all, only Haidar seemed to keep his head.

After a brief meal, Haidar rolled into his blanket on the rocky flat and pulled close to the fire they had made. Isfendiar stood the first watch. There would be no ambush prepared that night. They were too much in the open. More than once, though, Isfendiar pulled a brand from the fire and threw it at a moving shadow, but whether it was the bear or not he did not know.

In the morning they ate the last of the meat. Haidar

did not seem rested. His face had a pinched look. They would have to kill meat that day, he said.

"Is it the bear that makes you so solemn?" Isfendiar asked when they were taking the day's first steps.

"Yes, the bear, Little Friend. My old musket is useless against it except at short range. We must ambush the monster or else perish, it seems to me."

That day Haidar walked without talking, choosing carefully so as not to be misled again. They halted frequently. The sickness of the snows was still in Isfendiar's soul. Once close to midday, in the forest again, Isfendiar found himself standing beside a stream kicking in stones, while Haidar called from two hundred yards away, unheeded. How long he had been standing like this he did not know. He knew only that as he turned and walked, the thoughts of the eternal snows of the mountains muffled his mind and slowed his feet.

"Yes," said Isfendiar, and he heard his voice ring out lifelessly in the quiet air of the mountainside. "And if the bear comes, you will shoot him?"

"Aye," said Haidar in the manner of the North. "You had better pray that I do, for if I do not kill it, how can you defend yourself?"

Isfendiar thought, and thoughts seemed to roll only slowly through his head. He was tired to death, and the ground seemed to roll under him where he sat, like the floor of men's motor machines that ran between the cities. "I know not," he said finally. "I have a knife."

"A knife against a killer bear," said Haidar, not

laughing. "It is not much."

"I will let him draw me to him," said Isfendiar. "I have seen men do this. And I will have the knife against my chest so that his strength pulls it into his heart."

"You can be hurt," said Haidar. "You could die easily doing that."

"Yes," said Isfendiar. His thoughts whirled and rolled in his head. Nothing seemed to make any difference. Life was a false thing, a fiction that one tangled up through one's own devices. He should be tending the kilns many hundreds of miles to the south, yet he walked behind a northerner, almost an outlaw really, waiting for a bear they were going to try to kill.

Later in the afternoon, Haidar found the kind of place he was looking for and they stopped. Haidar hid, and Isfendiar sat out in plain view, the bait for the bear. Isfendiar sat with his thoughts and knew he had been dreaming again, for it was a shock when he heard almost simultaneously, the click of gravel under some heavy object and the click of Haidar's musket being made ready. He could see nothing. The mountainside towered over the forests as before. The sun had gone well behind the farthest range. Only a few birds broke the stillness. Yet there had been the noise of gravel being shuffled, and Isfendiar knew that he had been listening to it for some time in a sort of trance. The snows had taken the life from him once again.

He reached slowly for his knife, and, as it came out, he heard and saw in rapid succession, Haidar jump to his feet, sight the musket, and fire a shot that seemed to knock the wind out of the whole world.

It seemed to Isfendiar that Haidar had fired directly at him. Of course, it was behind him at the bear that the guide had fired, but the noise of the bullet hit Isfendiar like the blow from a club. He half turned, half reeled, and rose drawing the knife. His legs almost gave way beneath him for being cramped, and in fear at seeing the monstrous shape silhouetted against the darkness of the slope.

It was a dream, all the dream of a winter's night, Isfendiar felt, as he heard Haidar fumbling with his musket and cursing loudly enough to be heard over the enraged grunting of the bear.

Now that Isfendiar had gained his feet and looked closer, he could see blood trickling from the bear's chest. There was the dreaded half-moon of white fur and the doggy, musty stink of bear. If Haidar had hit the heart, the bear would have fallen, but here he was, a few feet away, sniffing his way toward his enemies.

The bear seemed almost blind, Isfendiar noticed in those split seconds. He looked to one side, grunting and sniffing with his huge snout. He wiped the air with one paw, smashing at it so that the wind whistled. Then he lumbered rapidly towards Isfendiar. Isfendiar held his knife against his chest and took two short steps into the bear's arms, so that they caught him and crushed him to the bear's chest. Isfendiar managed to say God's name as the blow caught him, and then the thousand

lights of the snows grew in his head until light was everything, and then darkness.

A thousand years later, it seemed, he heard someone's voice calling him. It was Haidar. Poor Haidar had run into some trouble reloading his musket, and he, Isfendiar could no longer help. No, it was that Haidar was calling him back from somewhere. Haidar had need of him. Isfendiar pulled a breath to try to clear his head, and the pain in his ribs made him cry out. He heard Haidar's voice: "So, you are alive, little dove."

Isfendiar opened his eyes to see a world still whirling. He could make out Haidar's face near his and see his own chest covered with some heavy stinking warm fluid. It was blood. Of course, that was it, it was bear's blood. "Where is he?" he asked Haidar as he propped himself off the ground with a very weak and trembly arm.

"Over there, Little Wonder," said Haidar pointing.

Isfendiar looked, and one of the boulders turned magically into a massive dead bear right before his eyes. The dream grew together in his mind. There was the half-moon, so it was all true what he had dreamed. "It is as you say, Kind Friend," said Isfendiar. His voice seemed to gain in strength in spite of his ribs. "I have difficulty breathing," he told Haidar. "That monster has crushed my ribs."

"And small wonder, Little Friend," said Haidar. "You were like a mouse in the paws of a cat. They will not believe us when we tell them how you slew the bear. Many people have heard of killing a bear in this fashion,

54

but that is all folk tale, the talk of days gone by, when heroes rode the surface of the earth and men were giants."

"I can believe it, all right," said Isfendiar moaning. "I will not be able to walk."

"You must walk," said Haidar. "I will bind your ribs, and you will sleep for the night. In the morning you will be able to walk."

Haidar helped Isfendiar walk a few hundred yards to a spot where they could sleep. "Tomorrow will see us with friends," he said. And that is all Isfendiar could remember of that day, for he slept.

7

IN THE MIDDLE OF THE NEXT DAY they walked the final miles down the valley of the Syalen Rud, or River of Misery as it would be said in the South, and into a village. The town dogs nipped at their heels as they walked the muddy street. The dogs took them for beggars and even the townspeople looked at their rags and strained faces with more curiosity than behooves mountain people. Yet there was a welcome, and food, and a place to rest for the night. Isfendiar wanted no more than that.

When he awoke in the middle of the next morning, everything had been decided. Bearers and donkeys would be sent after the hunting party, but Isfendiar was to stay to tell the chief of the hunt and to stand in place of the chief's son who was to lead the bearers. They were to go through the Garmedar pass to Alamut Rud, thence up the slopes of the Eagle. Haidar would have none but the chief's son as a leader, and the chief would have Isfendiar as a mock-hostage. "This is the land of the Assassins," said the old chief, "and the boy will stay with me and tell me about the bear."

So, shortly before noon Isfendiar watched a train of men and mules go up the road that turned shortly into a muddy trail and then to a mere pathway.

Haidar seemed to be footsore, but he was cheerful. The villagers whom he took along were eager for adventure. What better way of spending a week in the Moon of the Hunt, particularly if there were city men with money to share with them. The men of the town wore their rude skins and felt hats. Their shoes were made from goatskin and wood. Isfendiar watched the group pull slowly up the southern slope above the town and disappear into the hills.

The second night in the village was strange. Isfendiar's sleep was haunted with snowthings, impossible ugly animals that scampered in the field of brass-hands. The things that men said turned to uglinesses in the thin air of the snows. He woke more than once.

"Do you dream of the bear?" the chief asked in the morning.

"Aiee, not of the bear, Honored Friend. Of the snows and things that should not be."

"Where is your home?"

"In the desert of the South."

"Ah, you are a plainsman." There was a mixture of

contempt and envy in the speaker's voice. "You are not used to the wildness of our mountains. Things here are strange to you and you think they do not trouble you, but the soul wonders and is appalled at the variety of things."

"You speak like a poet."

"Not as a poet, but as one who knows poetry."

"Do you know that saga of Krisna? It is one of Firdousi's most magnificent."

"Of course." And part of the nights were spent in reciting the cantos of the epic poetry. "You will be well again when you get home," the other told Isfendiar. "That is where you will make your soul whole again."

And it was true, Isfendiar reflected. He had thought of himself as a man who could walk the face of the earth bravely. But there were voices calling him back to the plains of his birth, and his heart would be warmed by seeing his people and his country again. It was time to return to the South and look into the eyes of his friends again. There were those who had said that he should take a wife for the restlessness. Maybe they were right. Maybe a wife and children were something to build upon and to keep the soul from fainting in the still reaches of the desolate night. Yes, he had killed, and he was a man. Maybe he should speak to his father when he returned.

"Come now," said the chief one evening. "That youngest daughter of mine. The one with the black eyes who smiles when she sees you and laughs when you talk.

She is yours with a hundred toman to take to your father." The chief paused and puffed on his pipe. "Think carefully, for this can make your life among your people."

"I am not of blood," said Isfendiar. "I am a charcoal-burner's son. My blood is not the blood of chiefs but the blood of the soil."

"Eh? Is it so?" said the chief wonderingly. "From whence these feats, then?"

"I know not," said Isfendiar, for there was no way of denying that there had been feats. "Except that my father in his wisdom named me after a great king."

"You hold with your father, then?" asked the chief.

"As is God's will," replied Isfendiar.

"Then my daughter is not for you, though I look with respect on your blood."

"Nay," said Isfendiar, laughing in the dialect of the South. "It is that women's noise and smiles and gibes and perfumes and candies would make me ill in a week. It is said in the South, 'How can the daughter as the mother does not?'"

"Aiee," said the chief, "it is said in different words here. And how can you, a lad, expect to rule one of these silly useless animals when he sees the old chief in his wisdom being made a fool? You are right. Find a desert woman to keep your hut, and leave jewelry to the chief."

And then the chief told a story: There was a man of Khorammshahr who fell upon bad times in a city distant from the place of his birth. He was old and ill, and he had no money, no place to stay. So in the manner that God permits poor people, he put himself in the street to ask help from wayfarers.

One day a child shared a prayer-cookie with the poor man, and, as it happened, this was witnessed by a rich man, one of the city elders.

"How dare you soil the streets of this great city with your presence?" cried the rich elder. "This is a city of commerce. Caravans must pass where you stand. Nobles will look from their windows, and you will afflict their eyes with your poverty."

"It is that I have need," said the poor man. "I am old and sick. I am so poor that I cannot eat, let alone set foot for the place of my birth. So I ask for help from my brothers and sisters under God."

"Dirt!" cried the rich man. "You are wasting the time of one of the most important men in the city. And you have the gall to be without shame."

The poor old man looked sadly upon his fellow human. He took the piece of prayer-cookie he had wrapped so carefully, and thrust it into the pocket of the rich man. "Brother," he told the rich man. "Take this, for those with eyes know that you have greater need of God's love than I."

No, it was not a wife and family that he needed, Isfendiar reflected, looking into the short-lived embers of the fire of mountain shrubs. The fire had burned down, as it always would. If one could not be a man alone, how could he be a man to his family?

The question he had brought with him from the South was eternally with Isfendiar. And now, talking with the chief, it haunted the back of his mind. In the faint strands of smoke rising from the coal were the twisted thoughts from the mountains, the brass hands, the huge print in the snow that marked the bear, the infinite snows. Were these things merely things that troubled a mind that had not learned to be humble before God?

In a little while the question spoke itself from Isfendiar's lips as if he had not phrased the thought. "What does one say to a vain child?" Isfendiar asked the chief. "A child so vain that he cannot see the road to happiness in God's world?"

The chief seemed to suddenly come awake. He looked narrowly at Isfendiar, grunted, then threw his head back with laughter.

"I see you do not mean me," he roared. "You put the question without malice. Then I shall tell you another story."

"There is a story of Mount Demavend," the chief said in a voice that signified he was somewhere else, thinking of another person, maybe the person who had told him the story.

"And what is it, Dignified One?"

"It is simply this: A rich man from Shemiran went into Tehran to the poor quarter. And surprised to see that the same mountain that made its appearance for him in Shemiran was also there in the poor quarter of

Tehran, he asked a peasant which mountain it was."

" 'The mountain of the skies, Father,' replied a poor man.

" 'And could you climb it?'

" 'Not such as I. Could you? How long would it take you?'

" 'But a day,' said the rich man. And he set out to climb Demavend.

"At the end of the first day he found the mountain undiminished before him. He put it down to his eyes. They deceived him. Surely on the next day the mountain would vanish beneath his feet.

"At the end of the next day the mountain seemed still to tower. It would be finished on the next day.

"And so it went. Each day the rich man claimed it would be the end."

"But what happened then?" Isfendiar was impatient.

The chief waved a hand. "He is still there, a prisoner of his own vanity."

A typical mountain story. Isfendiar was sure the chief was laughing at him. But no, he was gazing into the fire, still lost in the same world of the past. And yet the story could not be true. How very strange. It was enough to make one wonder.

On a cold morning in the last days of the year, the party from the mountain arrived in the village. They were all next to dropping from cold and hunger. The mules had had little fodder. The man with the broken leg rested in the chief's house. He was feverish and called for his wife. Haidar spoke with Isfendiar. "I will take the city men down to Tanakabum," he said. "Khurramabad, as you lowlanders call it, being ignorant of things. They can find transport there, and I can go back to my town."

Isfendiar was sad. The mountain man was telling him that the hunt was over and he would have to go his way. The worthy Haidar seemed at a loss for words. "I have not fared badly," Isfendiar told the mountain man. "I have learned, and I have seen more of the nature of things. Above all I have your friendship."

Haidar did not smile. "The city men say they have little money to give us. They promise to send it by courier, but I do not believe it. How will you find your way home with no money?"

"I am like the jackal," said Isfendiar smiling. "I find my way at night. But what of you? With your family and your children?"

"Ah, it is bad."

"Why do you not ask for one of the rifles? You could sell it in one of the villages."

"The very thing, little man from the South." Haidar's eyes lit, then narrowed. "We will demand rifles."

"But let the chief do it for you. He is versed in these things. Tell him what the matter is about."

In the late afternoon the chief called the guides and the city men to his hut. Isfendiar watched the old man explain that a bargain was a bargain, and that money should pass from hand to hand.

The city men said that there was no money, that they would send it back with a courier.

Then the chief stood up. "So be it," said he. "And since you are honorable men, you will not be angry with a poor foolish village chief who has had your rifles taken from your luggage. These rifles will remain until money has been paid."

The city men sat with mouths open. They had not expected such treatment. How much money would it take to buy the rifles so that they could travel with them? they wanted to know.

"The amount you promised to pay the guides and the bearers. Presents for all. Gratuities for those who had helped, and a penalty to the chief of the village." It came to some hundreds of rials.

The city men hemmed and hawed. A wallet came out and banknotes. In a few minutes the sum was on the table.

"You said you had no money," said the chief.

"Insufficient for the trip home," said the fat one, smiling.

"Well, God grant that you do not starve," said the chief, smiling back now.

In the morning the party broke up, Haidar taking the city men to Khurramabad, and the bearers returning to their villages. Everyone was tired and sad to part company. The money in the men's pockets did not cheer them.

8

ISFENDIAR SAID HIS FAREWELLS in the village. He would climb to the Garmedar pass, thence to the river valley and to the Talaghan pass. He felt it an easy walk, now that he was a mountain man. He would take a little cloth of food, some matches, and his two good feet, and make the trip.

"And do you not fear traveling without a rifle?" asked the chief.

Isfendiar pointed to his knife. "It has done well for me."

"You shall have a rifle in the manner of a man," said the chief. "When you arrive at Ashnistan, you can leave it with the head man."

"How is it you take it upon yourself to do such kindnesses to the son of a charcoal-burner?" Isfendiar wanted to know. He was really teasing the old chief.

"Respect infants," said the chief, not smiling overmuch. He was sad to see his friend go. "Yes, respect infants, for they shall be your guardians when you are old."

"It is well spoken," Isfendiar said.

"And you have money for your trip?"

"More than twenty rials. But I care not for that. I bring away far more in wisdom and kindness."

"And are you so wrapped in a woolen garment that you scorn money?"

"I need only a little rice. The rest I will send to my father when I reach Kasvin. The Government man in the Post Office does it for you. It is all very scientific. The money goes along the wire. It was explained to me."

"If you so scorn riches, what will you say when I give you a jewel?" asked the chief, drawing a gold-mounted sapphire from his clothes. "Give it to the father of the girl you choose. He is the one who must be your friend."

Isfendiar laughed. "I have no need for such things."

"Of course not," said the chief, smiling again. "You are Sufic, a mystic, wrapped in a woolen hood. But take it to please a foolish old man."

The chief drew Isfendiar to him, embraced him, and pushed him out the door, being unwilling to listen to the boy's thanks. Isfendiar was alone on the road leading out of the village.

Isfendiar shot a deer on the river side of Garmedar pass. The rifle the chief had given him was accurate and easy to carry. Isfendiar cut what meat he could carry,

then put the carcass in ice so travelers could find it if they got there before the wolves. The way to the Talaghan pass was open through the snow, and the walk down to the Chala pass, the road to Dasgird and Ashnistan, was simple to the new strength in Isfendiar's legs. And the long days gave him time he needed to consider all he had seen and heard. It could truly be said, he reflected, that there was as much wisdom and learning in the North as in the South, if a man had a will to discover it.

The rifle he left in the headman's hut in Ashnistan when he came there. He was in Ashnistan on a morning, and in the evening he was in Kasvin, his ears ringing with the sound of the city.

At the Post Office Isfendiar had to explain how he had come by such a large amount of money. The clerk was apologetic when Isfendiar told him about the hunt and the bear. "There are so many thieves," he said.

The money was sent to the desert village. "I shall be there in three days," Isfendiar told the clerk.

"How can you go if you do not keep money for the bus?" the clerk wanted to know.

"I need only money for rice. I shall help the drivers of trucks, and they shall carry me."

And so it was. Isfendiar rode on rice trucks and beet trucks. In Tehran he found an oil truck going to Isphahan. Then south to Shiraz and east to the desert. It took a week.

In the village Isfendiar found himself in the middle

of a crowd of very excited people. Everyone had something to say, it seemed. But the young man would have none of it until he spoke with his father. The old man was at the kilns, everyone said.

Isfendiar found his father unloading one of the kilns. The piles of charcoal did not seem so much larger than when he had left. The brickwork on one of the kilns had fallen. Evidently it was not being used.

The charcoal burners gathered around as Isfendiar approached his father. "So goes the gazelle," said one of them, speaking lines from the poets. "Today in the desert, tomorrow in the hills."

Isfendiar's father did not look up when the young man approached. "It is you, as I have heard," said the old man. He moved slower among the brickwork and piles of charcoal, Isfendiar noticed.

"It is I, as you have heard," said Isfendiar. He saw both sadness and happiness in his father's words.

"We have used your money, it has done much. Have you had adventures?"

"Speak of me as a man from Mazandaran," said Isfendiar half laughing. "I have killed with my knife in Mazandaran. I was blooded there."

The Patient One stood up and looked carefully at his son. There was the same shrewdness in the old man's eyes. "And have you learned anything?"

"I have learned what to say to the vain child."

"And what is that?"

70

"You must ask the child what to do with a vain child."

"So you came by the answer."

"It was not I. I had to ask far and wide."

"Still, you came by the answer; that was not vanity. I am content."

"Then I am content too, Honorable One."

"And I am content to have such a son. Welcome home, Isfendiar. Welcome home, Son. Welcome home Isfendiar of Mazandaran."

The next morning, when candles were still lit, Isfendiar walked with his father to the kilns. The money had changed little in the village. They had a day's work ahead. No, the charcoal was not being bought, but someday it would be, and the fact that it would be bought someday made the work useful. A man needed useful work, Isfendiar said, otherwise why would his father walk like the others to the kilns, when now he was old enough to let others do the work.

While the shadows were still long, Isfendiar walked with his father in the cool hush of the desert. The sands and the hills beyond were peerless in their beauty. Each day the desert changed and returned upon itself, timeless. A man's life was but a moment in the time of all things, but in the desert the eternal could be found.

The day is short, Isfendiar said to the faint morning noises. One is barely awake when it is time to go to sleep. Let a man be brave in the sun, then. Let each day be an adventure in learning from God's Creation. Let

71

a man not fear to make mistakes in searching for the Way. If a man can put aside his vanity, he will be able to take his brother's hand.

Isfendiar drank the sweet air of the awakening desert. He felt his father's hand on his shoulder. He was home.